REVISITED
MEMORIES

PHILIPPE EVRARD
WITH
JOYCE PETERS

REVISITED MEMORIES

iUniverse books may be ordered through booksellers or by contacting:

iUniverse
1663 Liberty Drive
Bloomington, IN 47403
www.iuniverse.com
1-800-Authors (1-800-288-4677)

ISBN: 978-1-4917-6764-1 (sc)
ISBN: 978-1-4917-6765-8 (hc)
ISBN: 978-1-4917-6766-5 (e)

Library of Congress Control Number: 2015907321

Print information available on the last page.

iUniverse rev. date: 07/29/2015

CONTENTS

INTRODUCTION

While on a trip to Belgium during the winter of 2009, Joyce Peters was introduced to Philippe Evrard by a mutual friend. During conversation, Joyce and Philippe discovered they both had a mutual love for writing. Joyce had written poetry for many years, and in recent years some of her poems had been published. At the same time Joyce was writing poetry in the United States, Philippe was in his country of Belgium writing short stories from his actual life, beginning at a young age.

Joyce and Philippe exchanged e-mail correspondence periodically, and before Christmas of 2011, Joyce received a story from Philippe titled "Black-and-White Christmas." Philippe had written this story years before in French during the time of World War II. He remembered many happenings from the impressionable age of six. Years later, Philippe rewrote the story in English for his family and friends to read.

Secretly, Philippe dreamed of having his stories published in the United States and continued to write stories inspired by things he saw and experienced during his day-to-day life. Joyce eagerly read the story and was very impressed with the way Philippe described things that had happened during the war, in colorful and imaginative clarity, while holding her absorbed interest. After reading the story, Joyce immediately wrote to Philippe to praise his insight and description of what he remembered as a boy. She encouraged him to have the story published.

Philippe laughed and told her okay. "I appoint you as my personal editor."

Realizing that Philippe was serious, Joyce began inquiring about publishing companies that would be interested in possibly publishing a book for Philippe. Meanwhile, Philippe was eagerly rewriting other stories from French into English. Philippe sent other charming and interesting stories to be combined with "Black-and-White Christmas."

iUniverse was interested in publishing Philippe's stories in one book as a short-story collection. Philippe's excitement was infectious; Joyce helped with the rewriting and getting the stories to the publishers. She was excited for Philippe and proud and happy to help him fulfill his dream.

Unfortunately, Philippe became sick in the spring of 2012. After numerous tests, visits to the hospital, and some surgery, Philippe was diagnosed with terminal cancer. Joyce did not initially know the severity of Philippe's illness and continued to write e-mails encouraging Philippe to fight to get well, telling him he had the book to look forward to, asking various questions about certain characters in stories, and learning what certain French words meant.

Joyce was so very shocked and devastated when he wrote to give her the news. After a day of thinking and wondering what to do, Joyce threw herself into writing and corresponding with the publishing company, trying to speed the possibility of getting the book published in the hopes that Philippe would realize his long-awaited dream. Joyce promised Philippe that she would do everything in her power to see his stories published.

Sadly, Philippe did not live to see his dream fulfilled. After a short time, Joyce received an e-mail from Philippe's daughter Laurence who also lives in Belgium. Laurence was instrumental in helping gather other stories her father had written, information about her father, and family pictures. She also had a great interest in getting her father's stories published. With Laurence's unwavering help, the book became the long-awaited treasured collection of true stories written by her father, Philippe Evrard.

Joyce feels humble and thankful to have had the pleasure of befriending such a talented man who obviously possessed a witty and memorable personality, with a true and wonderful zest for life. He lived it to the fullest. Thanks to Philippe, his stories are a lovely legacy to his family and friends. He will live on through his own words, read by many in the United States and in Europe. He would have been so very proud to have his stories published in a beautiful book in the United States.

BLACK-AND-WHITE CHRISTMAS

It was World War II.

We lived in my grandparents' house in a small village in Belgium. It was my grandparents, my parents, my older brother, myself, and Marie-Louise and Pierre, sister and brother of my mother, Gaby.

Sometimes Céline came to our house for a visit. She was a friend of Marie-Louise.

In our village, life was concentrated around the church, the school, many farms, and a small factory that processed beets to produce sugar. My grandfather worked at the factory as a chemist. We lived just in front of the church. It was a very good observatory, we thought.

My younger brother came two years after the war. My father liked to tell the story of his birth. The baby was born at home in the small hours of the morning. Being a civil servant, my father left the house for work in the morning. He told the neighbors, "We have a little black at home," meaning the baby had very dark hair.

War was not far behind, so the neighbors mistakenly understood that the baby had an African American father.

In our village there were three important people: the priest, the mayor, and the teacher. I could add the taxi driver because he had a car.

The priest was an old man living with his sister, who seemed to be his mother.

The mayor could have been a character in an interesting novel.

The teacher was also a composer and singer. After the war, he composed many "opérette's" for soap operas, which were real blockbusters in Wallonia, the French-speaking part of Belgium, as everyone knew it. The teacher was not invited to Hollywood, but he could have been because of his extraordinary talent.

As a singer he would sing "Minuit Chrétien," or "Holy Night," each Christmas at the midnight mass. The lyrics were composed in 1843 by Placide Coppeau, a French wine merchant and poet. The music was the work of an unknown composer, Adolphe Adam. It is unfortunate that today the two men have been completely forgotten; however, their music is a must every Christmas in most churches in Belgium and other countries.

The Allied forces came to our Belgian village on September 6, 1944. First we received the British officers in our home. They spent most of the time sitting in the dining room, sipping cups of hot tea on white tablecloths.

My grandfather once said, "They act as if they were in India." Here they were not hiding from the sun but rather the cold and the snow.

When they quit the house, it was a relief to everyone.

Then came the Americans in jeeps, trucks, and command cars, with chocolates for the children. It was November when the Americans named Tommy and Walter came. They were much friendlier and became part of the family. They would play with the children, and I remember them pulling the wooden sled on the snow.

My parents invited the captain to dinner along with the most attractive girl in the village at that time. I remember precisely that we ate Belgian pommes frites. Even today I have the feeling that they were a little overcooked.

My brother and I became very possessive of our American soldier friends. My brother said Walter was "his American," and I wrote on the back of Tommy's photo, *Tommyesmonamerican*, all in one word (Tommy is my American).

I almost forgot to say that on the Genot's family farm, at the bottom of the church, there was a kind of jail in which some American soldiers were kept as some sort of punishment for unknown misbehavior. They could not leave the village without the captain's special clearance.

Christmas was in sight.

"Do you know," asks Félicien, my grandfather, "if Paul is going to be in better shape?" He spoke of our teacher, composer, and singer. "He did not leave the house for weeks. I saw him yesterday behind his window completely dressed with a hat, coat, and yellow scarf, but he did not move. He lives all day inside, dressed as though he were going out for a walk."

Of course, coal for heating was scarce, and many people lived fully dressed with coats inside their houses.

"I hope he will be able to sing our 'Minuit Chrétien,'" he added.

"If not," said Marie-Louise, "it will be as if the Germans were still here. And there were two casualties in the village …"

"And you were nearly arrested," said Gaby, my mother.

"Arrested?" asked Céline, who had just entered the room with her arms full of Christmas roses to decorate the church alter.

"Yes," my grandfather answered. "You don't remember last December when they came to steal the church bell?"

"And what was going on?"

"While they were lowering the church bells from the tower, a German looked through our bedroom window and saw Gaby taking a picture down from the wall."

"And then?"

"The Feldgrau came to the house and asked to go to the bathroom. I was on the stairs and said, 'What do you want?' He said, 'Photos.' 'Photos?' I replied. 'There are no photos here.' And I pushed him back down the stairs. He fell to the floor …"

"And what happened next?" asked Céline.

"Nothing. He went out, politely closing the door."

"How would you explain that?"

"I think I made it very clear that he was not invited …"

"Perhaps he was a coward."

"The very next day a lady came. As they loaded the bells onto the truck, she began to shout and insult them … They did not respond and stayed seemingly calm. The next day an officer came and asked the mayor who the woman was. He said he wanted to have her arrested.

"'Oh, I know this woman,' said the mayor, who was the notary. 'This woman is a fraud … She came here from Liege by the tram to collect food.' But in fact the woman who had insulted the Germans was his own wife."

"So you were lucky?"

"Yes, I must admit that I was really lucky. Listen, boys, don't do like me if another war should occur. Einverstanden."

"Anything else?" asked my brother.

"And what about Paul?" asked Céline.

"He is all the time fully dressed—hat, coat, and yellow scarf—behind his window. Looking for what, we don't know. Sometimes," said grandfather, "a prisoner whose name is Tommy pays him a visit … I asked myself if Paul is not trying to learn English."

"I already began," I said. "Tommy has taught me to count to ten, and I would like to go to the farm and learn more."

"It is enough," my mother said. "And those prisoners, we don't know what they have done."

"Yes, but there are ten of them, so I could learn to count to one hundred."

Christmas Eve came, and Paul was seen all day with his hat, coat, and yellow scarf on, behind his bedroom window. He never got out. Everybody began to get anxious.

"It is a shame," said our neighbor Clément. "We are now free, and for the first time since the World War we are going to a midnight mass without Paul singing our 'Minuit Chrétien.'"

In our village, as elsewhere, the good Christians had assigned places in the church. We were in the fourth row, on the right aisle, to use the company's terminology. If our great-grandparents had offered one of the churches stained-glass windows, we could have been sitting in the second or third row. Between the two main aisles there was a large corridor with two big stoves burning charcoal for heat.

Happily, we were on the side of one of them. Nevertheless, our feet were cold despite the fact that the fourth row had a wooden floor. Behind us the floor was made of stone and therefore colder. Also on each side of the church were two lateral aisles reserved for people who came for Christmas, Easter, and Assumption.

Now the mass was running fast, and the end was in sight. Suddenly, the carpenter began to move to his machine, but at first he did not play "Minuit Chrétien." It was not, I am sure, a Bach toccata … Nobody had heard this music before.

But some seconds later, the organ began to play Adolphe Adam music, and a golden voice fell from the tribune to the audience and began to sing, "Minuit Chretien, C'est l'heure solennelle."

> *Midnight Christmas, it is the solemn hour*
> *When God-man descended to us.*
> *People kneel down, wait for your deliverance.*
> *Christmas, Christmas, here is the redeemer.*

"I began to shiver," Céline later said. "I don't know why, but … tears came to my eyes. I cannot explain. I cannot explain. I do not find the words. It was so unexpected, and so great, so magnificent … I will never forget it. It was magnificent," she said again.

All the audience was now looking back at the tribune as the song continued.

> *The entire world thrills with hope*
> *On this night that gives a savior.*

After the mass, Marie-Louise would say, "He sang beautifully. He sings much better than Henry Garat." Henry Garat, a French singer of the '30s, was her idol, and she was in love with a man who looked like Henry Garat.

As the song was finishing, the organist put the light on, and the audience could see that Paul had given his yellow scarf to Tommy, the black prisoner, who had performed "Holy Night" in his place.

Probably for the first time ever, the entire church burst into spontaneous and continuous applause, which ceased and then resumed when Paul appeared near Tommy. Paul retrieved his yellow scarf, which he would later give to Tommy as a souvenir of this 1944 Christmas in the tiny Belgian village not very far from Bastogne.

During the mass, the snow had fallen heavily on the village. Pierre took me on his shoulders. Remember, I was six, and the snow was up to my waist.

"*Magnifique, un vrai Noël blanc,*" said Marie-Louise.

"A black singer," said Gaby. "Why not a black priest?"

"Yes, why not a black priest?" asked Céline. "But please, wait until after my funeral …"

Back home, grandfather said, "What a surprise. It was great … a truly great black singer. We have a true black-and-white Christmas," he added, "but no whisky at all, unfortunately."

"It is a pity that Walter hasn't come back," said Pierre. "This morning he promised me he would come back tonight with a bottle of whisky."

At that moment, we heard the characteristic noise of Walter's command car. He entered the room and placed his pistol and a bottle in the middle of the table.

"Big battle in the Ardennes," he said. "A true bloodshed, many casualties, many wounded. We don't see how to get out of this war." Opening the bottle, he sighed. "Yes, a black Christmas, a true black Christmas."

When my brother Michel read this story he told me that when Walter came back from Bastogne (the Battle of the Bulge), he placed his pistol on the table and took from his trousers a handful of medals, decorations, and insignias taken from German corpses.

It is understandable that this has not been mentioned in the story. One does things at one time that one would not do at another time.

Also, Céline died at the age of eighty-nine. As I write this story, I remember her saying, "A black singer, yes, and why not a black priest?" Being prejudiced, she really did not want a black priest in the village. But I observed at her funeral mass that there was indeed an African priest at the foot of her coffin.

During segregation the black soldiers were not in the same camp with the white soldiers, therefore, the people of the Belgian village thought the black soldiers were prisoners. Fortunately today we are all considered equal.

Josep set un
nammericin
sel til un prusognec.

TEXAS PECAN TREES

Barbara Against the Big Utility

"I have a farm," she said when I met her for the first time."

"In Africa?"

"No," she replied. "I am not Karen Blixen! She had a farm in Africa, but myself, I have a farm in Texas."

"Oh!" I said. "And so you don't grow coffee?"

"Not at all. I inherited the farm from my grandparents. When they bought it, they planted pecan trees. The trees are still there, more than one hundred years old!"

"And you like it?" I asked.

"Oh, so much," she answered. "It is my life."

"Are pecan trees very common in Texas?" I asked.

"Oh yes," she replied. "You can find pecan trees everywhere in this country."

Pecan is from an Algonquian word meaning a nut requiring a stone to crack.

"Do you think," I asked, "that General McAuliffe was thinking of the pecan trees when he replied 'nuts' to General von Luttwitz during the Battle of the Bulge in December of 1944? General von Luttwitz was pressing McAuliffe to surrender."

"Oh, I am sure," she said, "because the pecan trees may live and bear edible nuts for more than three hundred years, and McAuliffe was determined to resist, if necessary, more than three hundred years."

"And do you have problems with your trees?" I finally asked.

"Yes, the problem is that I have a farm of pecan trees that is not endangered by the Germans but by a big utility gas company. During World War II, my parents accepted an easement letting a gas company lay a pipeline across their property. It was during the war, and my parents were adamant to do something that appeared useful at the time. But the time has passed; there was never a single accident on the line, but now the gas company wants to clear out part of the property to make access easier in the possibility of fire, explosions, or other catastrophes."

"And you don't agree?"

"Of course not, but the fact is that they are eager and ready with trucks, cranes, and all their machinery to enter my property and cut six of my oldest trees."

"Haven't you an attorney?"

"I have a bunch of attorneys," she replied, "but you know billing is their specialty. Fighting on the ground is not …"

"Why fighting on the ground?"

"Because while the attorneys are arguing before the judge, the machinery could come and cut my trees in half an hour. Of course the gas company would be condemned to pay me punitive damage and so on. But it is not what I want. I want my trees on their feet, on my property, along my creek, where they are now. Nothing else."

"And what are you doing now?"

"I am going to resist with my golf clubs, my beloved John Deere tractor, my grandfather's rifle, my father's pistols, my pots, and if necessary, my life.

"You know," she added, "they asked me to surrender, but listen. I replied like McAuliffe, 'Pecan nuts,' and believe me they are not going to find in this country a stone big enough to crush my pecan head."

Three months later I came anew to her town to visit a customer of mine, but of course I wanted to know what had happened to the trees. When I came joyriding to her place, I saw immediately that the house was closed. The grass was not mowed, the barn was empty, and the John Deere was not to be seen. The farm seemed to be abandoned as if a war had raged through the vicinity. Even the cats, so attached to the place, seemed to have deserted.

To be sure, I decided to walk to the creek, where I knew the trees could be seen.

As I came in sight of the creek, I suddenly spotted a strange array of poles, ropes, and sheeting all intertwined around the beloved trees, making sort of a military base similar to the Vietnam War. On the top of it all, I see Barbara with two rifles in hand.

"Hands up," she said before recognizing who I was. She immediately came down the wooden ladder, firearms still in hand.

"Where are the cats?" I asked.

"They are in safe hands," she answered.

"Oh, good. I feared that they were taken hostage."

"No, they are cared for by the plumber."

"Nice of him … I came to see if I could help you."

"Nothing," she said. "You can't do anything for me, but perhaps I can do something for you."

"I don't know what," I said. "But I would gladly help you."

"You know," she said, "I am setting up a new business, a new consulting company called Fighting the Big Utility. I will provide everything: legal aid, media coverage, weapons, food, drugs—everything to support a siege—and a lot of tips to build an aerial den. Can I put you on my prospective clients list?" she asked.

"You know," I said, "I have no property endangered and, actually, no properties at all."

"Oh Jesus. Oh boy. Great, great, great," she said. "You are just the guy I was looking for. Listen … with my package—legal aid, media coverage, etc.—I am going to provide you a very lovely property that is really endangered by a big utility. I am going to help you buy it and find a loan so we will have the opportunity to fight the big utility together."

And saying that, she handed over one of her pistols to me.

"Really, isn't it great?" she asked.

"Yes, it is," I answered.

"But you seem to be scared," she said. "Don't be afraid. Trust me. I am going to help you. You know, it is not my first rodeo."

THE GIRL WITH THE HAT AND CIGARETTE

"I remember you perfectly," she said, "every morning at nine leaving the train station. You were with your friend and walking very fast on the right sidewalk leading to your first lesson of the day. I was on the opposite side, the left side, leading to the station. You were always staring at me as if I were a movie star or the queen of England, or a strange curiosity, though I am not sure what."

"Oh yes, I remember too," I said. "You were wearing a dark blue dress and flat shoes. You were always dressed like that. But after many months you did not appear anymore. My friend and I were very upset. We thought something bad could have happened to you," I said with a smile. "An abduction or something. Who knows?"

"Yes, it was a long time ago," she said.

Then she took from her handbag an old black-and-white photograph and said, "Have a look at this photograph."

In the photo there were two young men in their twenties and a girl wearing a dark dress, torn jeans, workers shoes, and a hat. In her left hand, the girl held a half-burned cigarette.

"Who is this?" I asked.

"Look very closely at the photograph," she said.

I recognized the girl with the hat and the cigarette, the one my friend and I were accustomed to seeing in the dark blue dress, the one who vanished one day and we did not know why.

"I do not understand," I said. "Why did you change your appearance at this time?"

"You know," she said, "I was very shy and became a discreet person. I was unsure and disturbed by the young men staring so intensely at me. So I decided to change my clothes to hide myself and dressed like a boy."

"Okay, but you could also have taken another street to avoid both of us," I said.

"Yes, but to be honest, I wanted to see you every morning," she said.

"Were you fond of us?" I asked

"Yes, I was," she answered.

"Which one of us?" I asked.

"Both of you," she said.

Oh …

DOGS PYRENEES

The gate is closed. There is no bell. Since I was invited by the landlady, I simply push the gate open and find myself on a driveway leading about half a mile farther to the big house. I feel uneasy because nobody is in sight, and I feel alone, watching my steps along the drive.

On the right, under an enormous tree, I see some pheasants feeding on insects. On the left everything seems to be very quiet except for the horses behind barbed-wire fences. Proceeding, I fear meeting a wild animal like a fox, a bear, or perhaps a gazelle because this is a hunting area. Some black ravens gliding on the canopy don't give me much confidence. Higher in the sky a helicopter is roaring.

After passing under orchards and along Greek statues, I arrive near a pool, and at my feet to the left I discover a big house. But it is not a big house; it is not even a mansion. It is a really old castle with turrets, like something straight from the Middle Ages.

To access the main entrance, I have to cross a yard paved with irregular cobblestones. As I move forward, I am on the verge of falling because the wet stones are slippery. I enter the yard and take several steps when all at once I see three, four, no … five oversized dogs coming directly from a barn with doors flung wide open. The dogs are quiet and very impressive, four feet high. I recognize their breed: Great Pyrenees.

They are all around me, sniffing at me. I don't dare move, not even to speak to them. I could possibly aggravate them, so I stay silent.

One of them says to another after sniffing my entire body, "No weapons," so they let me go. I then can breathe.

I am not far from the steps leading to the front door when suddenly I hear the barks of small dogs, no bigger than bichons, coming from the same barn. They yip, circling around me, and very soon try to bite my heels. Eventually they shout to the Great Pyrenees, "Come on! Something is wrong with him!" I am terrified. The Great Pyrenees do a U-turn and run to me with open menacing mouths.

I don't hesitate; I fly over the steps. Luckily the door is open, and I shut it behind me. I breathe anew. The Pyrenees drool with rage as I watch them from behind the glass door. They try to push the door open, but I have already locked it.

Inside, I see a very long and wide entrance hall furnished with tapestries and fine carpets on the floor. On the right, I see nobody in the kitchen. Silence. The dogs, having done their duty, are no longer barking. I feel that I cannot make noises, so I proceed by tiptoeing across the carpets.

I pass the dining room and the grand salon; the doors are open, but no one is there. The drawing room comes after the grand salon. The door is slightly open. I feel that there must be life behind the door and continue, feeling that I must keep silent.

Very cautiously I enter, craning my head around the half-open door, and see three little girls sitting on the carpet. Each one of them is caressing a baby kitten on her knee; the baby kittens are no bigger than mice.

One of them smiles at me and puts her finger to her lips.

We must not wake the sleeping kittens.

The girls' names are Amelie, Lucie, and Lisa, and I wish to be an artist to make a painting of them on a canvas.

My Neighbor's
Cat

He lives in a semidetached house next door to my office. He has lived there for ten years with the vet and his wife. A lady named Hatiou lives on the third floor and is the guardian of the house.

The two houses were built at the beginning of the nineteenth century and adorned in that period of style, with balconies and front gardens. The vet's façade and front garden were destroyed and replaced with an ugly yellow brick wall and a park place.

The vet owns a summer house on the island of Ibiza, the so-called paradise island located in the "mittle meer" that the Germans call the Mediterranean sea, which they specifically invaded.

The vet spends lots of time in Ibiza. That is, when his summerhouse is not rented to some German.

My neighbor's cat, Loviou, has never traveled to Ibiza with his owner. The cat said, "I don't like to ride to Spain, catch a boat, and arrive exhausted in Ibiza. I hate the plane, where you never have enough room for your legs. I don't like to stay in the sun, except in the winter garden. I prefer to stay home where I have my habits."

Cats, as everyone knows, are more attached to the location than to the person.

"You prefer to stay with Hatiou? And what about your health when your vet is sunbathing?"

"Of course I must care for him," he said. "And it is my interest to keep him in good health, in good shape, and if something happens to me, I shall call him back immediately."

So he stayed in the house with Hatiou.

She didn't like cats because they shed everywhere, especially on the stairs, on the carpet, on the tablecloth, on the kitchen table, on the sofas, and even in the bathroom if she didn't close the door.

In fact, the cat belonged to the house master, and the vet forbid him to go outside on the street, where he could have an accident and the vet could lose his valuable patient.

So Hatiou was supposed to maintain the cat inside the house and back garden, which was surrounded by a three-meter-high brick wall.

Hatiou disliked not only the cat but also the vet and his wife, who were never satisfied, always grumbling and finding something wrong in the house. It is also true that she hated the entire world.

She would not have been devastated if the cat was crushed under a lorry wheel or simply disappeared in the night. This last occurrence was the best. She left the front door open just long enough for Loviou to get out. She closed it immediately. No more bothering about him, she thought. Loviou was eager to get out to roam the street, to scent the walls and leave his mark on the cars like the dogs did. He was not accustomed to the noise, so he would sometimes retreat to my front garden and hide himself in the hortensias.

That was where we met on a Monday morning in September when the Ibiza summerhouse was not rented to a German couple. I couldn't tell his color because his hair was mixed and his eyes were dense black with golden rays.

He took the habit of waiting for me every day at 10:00 a.m. in the front garden. He would enter the house hurriedly through the stairs and wait for me in front of the door. Then he would rush to my armchair, where he would immediately pretend to sleep. I say pretend to sleep, because I realized after some weeks that he didn't sleep at all; rather, he was carefully listening and noting everything that was said and done in my office.

One day, not knowing what to do with a small case in my office, he said, "Don't waste your time with that trifle case. You have better things to do. Take the next file and work on it." He was right.

After that incident, I began to ask his advice about more complicated matters. I was astonished to see how quickly he assimilated to my job, and how meaningful his advice was. When I had a difficult explanation with a client and was trying to find a proper conclusion, I would propose and then ask for the cat's advice. I presented the whole thing like a joke, just to have a little fun so we could lighten the atmosphere and resume our arguments at a later time.

I realized that his advice was very well received by "our" clients, and this gave us enormous confidence in "our" business. So one Friday at 5:00 p.m., he left his chair, sat himself on my desk, and said, "Can we have a little talk?"

"Of course," I said. "Our week is nearly completed. We can have a little rest."

"I can't understand the way you run your business," Loviou said. "You are always driving everywhere; dictating letters and notes; and receiving urgent telephone calls that are not urgent at all. You study dull letters all day long. You dust papers for people who will have little reconnaissance of what you do for them. You look tired, you don't sleep well, and your lengthy digestions are making you a bad-tempered character. Really, it's not a living."

"You are probably right, but what can I do?"

"It is very simple," he said. "You must perform a U-turn, and in the first instance you must make the decision to give away what you call your 'bureautique.' Sell at once your telephone, fax machine, scanner, copier, printer, computer, iPhone, hard disk, and so on ... Have a clean desk without cords or cordless machines ..."

"How shall I work?"

"You must change your working routine completely. I don't want to say, for obvious reasons, that you must accomplish your Copernican Revolution. Forget this last expression ... No more telephones," he said, "means that the people must come and wait without a 'rendezvous.' All the ordinary gurus are acting like that. If you give rendezvous, you are just another practitioner. The people must wait. The more that are waiting, the more reliable you are."

He went on. "I cannot work if I am hungry. Our guests must bring something to eat," said the cat. "If I don't eat, I can't concentrate on the subject matter."

Loviou must be fed, I wrote on a paper that I left at the entrance door. *He is expecting to receive some food to sustain his poor health and convince you that he really loves you.*

So the first visitor came at seven in the morning with a plate and waited until nine or ten because Loviou would not get up earlier. He would smell the food, hesitate, turn around, and leave the room ... or eat it immediately. If he ate it, he would take a small nap afterward, before receiving the first guest.

"Tell him," he said, "that I am not going to do a very good job if I don't take a nap."

So the second guest waited until lunchtime to be received. For lunch, the cat made it clear that he wanted to eat *foie gras*, especially *foie gras des Landes* or *foie gras d' Alsace*. Having eaten an entire block of *foie gras*, after a small nap, he could listen better. He enjoyed listening with a full stomach.

"If your stomach is empty, you are tired; if you are tired, you need a good armchair or sofa. You cannot listen," he said.

Next he told me, "You have to empty your filing cabinets and give back all this paperwork to its legal owners."

"It is impossible to work without papers," I said.

"No. In the future you will give verbal advice only. No writing to do. Or reading … You are going to practice like a guru, giving advice only, good or bad omens. Leave the paperwork and the pleading to your colleagues. No, no more telephone, no more faxes. Just listening and giving omens for the future … without responsibility."

"I don't see myself acting like that …"

"If you want," the cat said, "I can help you at the beginning. I'll show you how to run your practice. You'll only have to watch me as I watched you all these last months."

So he sold all my "bureautique" and said, "You don't need those machines anymore. You don't need to buy another one, and so I retain the money for me. No use to you."

I found that once more he had an unexpected but logical point of view. I needed that.

I must recognize that it took several months to organize our new life and find a new type of clientele, or customer. We called them our "guests" or "visitors" because we were not using material at all. Once more, I was surprised by his careful daily organization and how he provided good advice.

"I cannot emphasize too much on this point," he said. "Some guests appeared with several kinds of pate, but without success. *Foie gras d'oie ou de canard*," he said in French, "are my *incontournables*."

Despite the fact that he only accepted three, or a maximum of four, guests a day, the number of visitors did not diminish. Everyone was eager to be received by Loviou.

Of course, we had some overhead. I had to pay the electricity bill … Loviou wanted air-conditioning working all year long …

So I asked him on Friday at ten o'clock, "Could we have a little talk together?"

"Sure," he said. "I will come after my nap."

I began to complain about the electric bill and other expenses … My own financial situation was getting worse and worse.

He didn't move. Then he closed his eyes and said, "Take this table and put it in the entrance. Fetch a plate from the cupboard over there. Place the pate on the table. Take this piece of paper and put it on the plate. Now write on the paper, *Your gift is welcomed*."

I tried to look at him to let him know what I was feeling, but he was already sleeping.

I did not dare wake him up.

Una Minus,
Christmas
at Jauche

The house is still there, at the very same place. At the entrance of the village. Now the new landlord has replaced the roof, changed the windows, cut down two big conifers that hid the house's façade, and installed new French doors overlooking the garden.

It looks narrow and very high because the parcel is narrow and long.

The garden is very large with lawns, vegetables, horse stalls, a garage for the carriage—and later the first Ford sold in the village—a meadow, woods, and trees, especially a large walnut tree. This house was built at the end of the nineteenth century (circa 1895) by a doctor, a physician, who at that time was still a bachelor.

When the construction was finished, he ordered brand new furniture for the dining room, drawing room, bedrooms, and kitchen from a Malines furniture manufacturer. This town was, and still is, renowned for its manufacturers.

It was a mistake to replace everything because he got married some years later to a daughter of a wine merchant who lived just in front of the newly renovated house. She eventually inherited a lot of exquisite old pieces of furniture that were redundant and stored for a century in the attics while the tasteless furniture bought by the good doctor remained in sight.

The wine merchant owned a very large property with wine cellars, greenhouses, meadows, a grot, and a garden surrounded by a high brick wall that was constructed by his grandfather when the Belgian state became independent in 1830. The man eventually abandoned the work somewhere in the middle of a field. Death, lack of money ... no one knew why he stopped. The Faimes' iron gate came from this wall, and the house was made with the bricks.

At this epoch, it was fashionable to have a grot in the garden, where the temperature was cool in the summer.

Unfortunately, the wine merchant's house fell into decay, and the wine cellars were completely abandoned and destroyed a century later by a fertilizer dealer.

The good doctor, who was also the mayor of the village for thirty years, was married and had three children, all born at the beginning of the century. His children were named Paul, Fernand, and Clara. Fernand was a bank manager. He met his wife, Marie-Therese, on a train to Luxembourg, where she lived before World War II. When they got married, they settled in Brussels, where Jacqueline was born in 1942. Fernand died of a heart attack at the age of fifty-eight in 1960.

Clara never married. She looked after her father, the good doctor, who died in 1953.

Paul was a Jesuit, a professor, a man larger than life, who taught and guided hundreds of students who saw him as a charismatic professor of literature, Greek, Latin, history, and philosophy. He loved life, friends, family, students, good food, and very old wine— the healthiest drink according to Pasteur himself. Paul lived in Brussels and came back to the family house for Christmas, Easter, Pentecost, Assumption (August 15), and the Feast of All Saints.

Clara cooked a great dinner with four or five courses: soup, appetizer, game, beef or veal with vegetables, and dessert. Around the table there was Clara, Paul, Marie-Therese, Jacqueline, Jacqueline's husband and three children, and a special guest ...

The special guest was the village priest.

He was called Monsieur le Curé.

Monsieur le Curé called Clara, Mademoiselle. He would call Paul, Père Goreux or Père Paul. He would also talk to Madame Goreux (Marie-Therese) or Jacotte.

Monsieur le Curé appreciated Paul's presence during the feast because he liked ceremonies with at least three priests, many choirboys, an organ, songs, banners, flowers, and the entire parish around him.

After the Holy Mass, around midday, Monsieur le Curé would bless the children at the church door, and eventually their group would come back for the five-course lunch.

"What a nice table, a fine tablecloth," said Monsieur le Curé upon entering the dining room, which was opened only three times a year. "We have never entered the drawing room, which is closed all the time."

"It's natural," answered Clara. "It's Christmas."

"Yes, it is Christmas, and I bring you some of my best wine, chosen especially by my friend Una Minus from my cellar."

Who is this Una Minus? Tante Clara asked herself. *Let's wait. Sooner or later we will learn who he is.*

"It was a great midnight mass," said Monsieur le Curé. "A mass with five horses—I mean, a mass with five priests … Nowadays it is nearly impossible to gather five priests at the same time and the same place."

"And five good horses," said Père Paul. "Among them was a young brother who came from a small community living in the next village, Jandrain. Where is he now?"

"Oh, Père Paul, he is unlucky. He is invited for lunch by the Jandrenouille's priest … He is going to eat sausage and potatoes and drink water, while we are going to appreciate the great mademoiselle's cuisine.

"Oh yes, we are lucky. A farmer brought a pheasant, and another one sent a hare, and Pierot fished for us a pike from the good sisters' waters … He is the only one who can fish on the property … With the Pierot's pike, we will drink a Pouilly-Fuisse 1959. I must say that I could also have brought a Liebfraumilch, but you know we are obliged to restrain ourselves. We can't enjoy all the wines at the same time. It is true, and I myself find this burgundy to be perhaps the best white wine I have drunk in my life. Not sour, not too sweet—a perfect blend."

Tante Clara came in with the pheasant and placed it in the middle of the table.

"To drink with the pheasant, Una Minus chose for us a Chateau Petrus 1959, a good Bordeaux. What else could you dream of to accompany this magnificent bird? Père Paul," said Monsieur le Curé, "my Petrus '59 is not a good Bordeaux; it is the best Bordeaux. Better than Cheval Blanc, the Pontet-Canet, or the Chateau Haut Certan of your friend Gerard."

"It's true, Monsieur le Curé. This is another wine … another category, despite my fondness for my friend Gerard."

After the fish and the pheasant, a hare was to come. The entire animal was served on a plate, and Père Paul began to carve and serve the hare while Monsieur le Curé was opening a bottle of Burgundy.

"With a hare and his very strong nature, we need a very strong wine," said Monsieur le Curé. "I chose an Aloxe-Corton '59 because it is the best year since the war, except 1947, and because I have nothing else other than 1959. All of my cellar is composed of 1959 wine and, according to my calculations, I can live ninety years without having to go to the supermarket to buy a bottle of wine."

"It is really great," said Paul. "I have never drunk such an exquisite Burgundy. *Quelle robe, quel vin puissant.*"

"Behold your superlatives for the end," said Monsieur le Curé. "My friend Una Minus could have a surprise for us."

"Who is this man?" asked Tante Clara.

"In fact, Una Minus is not a man. It is a Latin expression that means 'one less.' It is a good rule meaning that if we are for example six guests—I don't count the children—we are only entitled to drink one less. That means five bottles … Do you understand?"

"Yes, I understand. And why are you calling your friend Una Minus?" asked Clara.

"I like to call him that because he is always helping me to observe the rule … Oh, he is just coming to the front door with a box delicately carried in his arms. I have the feeling that he has in the box perhaps a bottle of Romanee-Conti or something like that."

"Now that he has come here among us, we have one more guest, and if he should carry a bottle, we could drink one more bottle," remarked Père Paul.

"You have a very quick spirit," said Monsieur le Curé, "so I give you a special degree in canon law, but what more is added is the fact that, sadly, my friend Una Minus is forbidden by his physician to drink one drop of alcohol. So he is very suited to carry my best wine, especially when it is a Romanee-Conti '59."

Una Minus entered the dining room. He had removed the bottle from the box and presented it in his arms like a newborn baby.

"Sit down, my friend," Père Paul and Monsieur le Curé said politely. "I am sure you are going to have a glass of wine with us."

"Monsieur le Curé," said Una Minus. "I suffer from diabetes, I have too much cholesterol, and my blood analysis is very bad. Son, I can only drink water ... and not too much of that."

"Oh, poor boy. You don't deserve such a fate."

"So, Monsieur le Curé," added Una Minus, "the doctor told me, 'My boy, you can't drink a drop of beer or alcohol. It is too dangerous for your health.'"

"Oh, it's a pity," said Monsieur le Curé. "At your age."

"Yes, he told me that, Monsieur le Curé, but you know, he added, 'You can't drink even a single drop of wine.'"

"Oh, poor boy."

"Yes, but you know, coming here, I met the doctor on the street. He saw the bottle and the box, and he said again, 'You can't drink a single drop of wine, except for the wine of Monsieur le Curé,' for his wine is much better for you than any drug. So, Monsieur le Curé, I think I can accept a taste of this wine with you, but you know the doctor told me, 'If it happens that Monsieur le Curé offers you some wine, don't drink more than half a bottle.' Yes, the doctor told me that."

DARK CHRISTMAS

24–25 Décembre 1944

- Est-il vrai que notre "instituteur chantant" souffre d'une extinction de voix ? demande Grand-père.
- Oui, il paraît qu'il ne peut plus dire deux mots tellement il est accablé, répond Marie-Louise.
- Il ne pourra pas chanter à la Messe de Minuit ?
- C'est à craindre.
- Quelle catastrophe! Une messe de Minuit sans un "Minuit Chrétien" ne sera pas une vraie Messe de Noël, dit Marie-Louise.
- Je lui ai conseillé de prendre trois petites gouttes avant et après chaque repas, dit Grand-père. Cela devrait le retaper. Je ne suis pas sûr qu'il suivra mon conseil, mais moi je garantis le résultat.
- A-t-il appelé le docteur ?
- Oui, mais le docteur dit qu'il lui faudrait de la pénicilline … pour l'instant seuls les américains en ont.
- Que peut-on faire ?
- Rien, si ce n'est prier.
- Quoi prier ? dit Maman; prier pour ce mécréant qui ne va à l'Eglise qu'une fois par an et encore pour chanter.
- Oui, mais pour chanter notre Minuit Chrétien, corrige Grand-père. Quelle voix, dès qu'il entonne le premier couplet, les larmes me montent aux yeux.
- Et moi, je ressens des frissons dans le dos, tellement c'est prenant, ajoute Céline qui passe par la maison après avoir porté des fleurs à l'église.

– Voilà huit jours qu'il ne fait plus la classe, ajoute Grand-père, et je me demande pourquoi ce Tommy est fourré deux fois par jour chez lui ?

– Qui est ce Tommy ?

– C'est un soldat noir aux arrêts de quartier.

– Un soldat à la peau noire, aux arrêts ?

– Oui aux arrêts. Je ne sais pas ce qu'il a fait, mais il est en punition à la ferme Genot. La ferme est devenue une sorte de prison. Ils sont là une dizaine. Ils n'ont plus d'armes et ne peuvent quitter le village. Et qu'est-ce que ce Tommy fait chez l'instituteur ?

– Mystères et boules de gommes ? Je ne vois pas très bien ce qu'ils peuvent se dire, à moins qu'ils ne s'écrivent. D'ailleurs, Paul ne connaît pas un seul mot d'anglais.

L'église est pleine à craquer. Cela n'arrive qu'aux grandes fêtes : Noël, Pâques, Pentecôte, quinze août. Il faut jouer des coudes pour arriver à son banc ou à sa chaise réservé. Il y a des privilégiés; notamment les familles qui ont des bancs réservés; certains sont même sont gardés par des portillons. Heureusement, les portillons ne ferment pas à clef. On n'a pas de portillon, mais on est tout près d'un poêle.

Il y a deux grands poêles à charbon au milieu du couloir central de l'église; ils sont rouges à craquer; ceux qui sont assis à côté meurent de chaud, tandis que ceux qui sont restés au fond de l'église ont froid aux pieds.

Tout le monde attend avec impatience la fin de la messe.

Surprise, l'instituteur est là. On peut le voir au jubé à côté du menuisier qui tient l'orgue. En effet, la paroisse peut s'enorgueillir d'avoir un menuisier organiste. On a aussi un accordéoniste, mais il n'est pas autorisé à jouer dans l'église.

Va-t-il pouvoir chanter « *Minuit Chrétien, c'est l'heure solennelle* …?

Papa n'hésite pas à se retourner et à inspecter le jubé. Il a l'habitude de se retourner dans l'église pour repérer les quelques personnes qu'il souhaite rencontrer à la sortie. Il est là, dit-il, mais Maman reste impassible. On ne se retourne pas à l'église.

Un silence plein d'interrogations se fait au moment crucial où la voix de Paul doit tomber du jubé sur l'assemblée qui attend ce moment depuis une bonne heure déjà.

Suspense. Chantera-t-il, chantera-t-il pas ? Que va-t-il se passer ?

L'orgue du menuisier se met à jouer les premières notes du Minuit Chrétien.

Chacun retient son souffle en anticipant les paroles dans sa tête ; *"Minuit Chrétien, c'est l'heure solennelle où l'enfant"*.

On craint le pire: que l'instituteur perde non seulement la voix mais encore la face.

- Il a une grosse écharpe jaune autour du cou, remarque Grand-père, c'est mauvais signe. Va-t-il enlever son écharpe ?

Puis, soudain, une voix surpuissante, pleine de couleurs, s'élève et remplit toute la nef de l'église dont la voûte semble subitement menacée d'écroulement.

"Minuit Chrétien, c'est l'heure solennelle où l'enfant dieu ..."

Les paroissiens sont comme pétrifiés ; ils n'osent pas se retourner craignant de mettre fin à ce qui ressemble à un vrai miracle.

- Il est capable d'aller jusqu'au bout ... pense Papa. Quel type ce Paul ... qui en dehors de la musique, ajoute-t-il mentalement, ne comprend rien à rien.
- Je n'ai pas tout de suite compris ce qui se passait, dira grand père. Il faisait tellement noir là-haut dans le jubé ...
- Moi, j'ai tout vu, dit Papa. Paul était à côté de l'orgue avec son manteau noir et son écharpe jaune. Il a commencé à chanter; en tout cas, il faisait semblant de chanter, mais je voyais bien qu'il y avait quelqu'un derrière lui. Il faisant tellement noir que je n'ai pas de suite aperçu le Tommy. Je ne l'ai reconnu que lorsque Paul l'a pris par le bras, l'a fait venir à sa hauteur et puis s'est effacé derrière lui. J'ai bien vu que c'était le Tommy qui chantait ...
- Je n'ai jamais rien entendu d'aussi beau dans ma vie, dit Marie-Louise. Je croyais que Paul avait retrouvé sa voix, mais la voix du Tommy est encore plus belle, plus chaude que celle de Paul ... et puis il a une telle puissance, une telle sonorité ... Oui vraiment, on n'a jamais eu un Noël comme ça.

- Ils ont fait une sorte de play-back, dit Oncle Pierre qui avait commencé à étudier l' "Anglais sans peine" début septembre.
- C'est une expression américaine; cela signifie qu'un chanteur fait semblant de chanter pendant qu'un autre chante à sa place ou qu'on diffuse un enregistrement, explique Pierre.
- C'est un peu comme un écrivain qui utilise un nègre, dit Grand-père feignant d'ignorer sa trouvaille, tandis qu'il se sert l'air de rien son deuxième « petit blanc ».

Dehors, le ciel s'assombrit, de gros flocons commencent à couvrir le jardin.

- C'est ça, corrige Grand-père, qui vient d'étudier à son tour la première leçon d'Assimil : on a eu droit à du Black et maintenant voilà du White … mais point pour autant de Black and White...
- Pas sûr, dit Papa, qui a tout de suite saisi, malgré sa méconnaissance totale des langues (sauf le Wallon), le commandant Walter est parti ce matin dans les Ardennes; il a promis de rentrer ce soir avec une bouteille de Whisky … dit-il.
- Pour autant qu'il revienne, dit Maman.

Elle n'a pas terminé sa phrase qu'on entend une Jeep s'arrêter devant la maison. Walter rentre dans la salle à manger plus blanc qu'un bonhomme de neige.

- Big battle in the Ardennes, dit-il en déposant son revolver et son ceinturon sur la table. Il ajoute en Français : "beaucoup morts, beaucoup blessés, beaucoup prisonniers, beaucoup blood".
- Yes, dit-il enfin, really it's a black Christmas.

L'ASCENSION

– Mademoiselle, je suis las d'entendre votre neveu nous parler de courants ascendants, de cumulus, de stratus, de cumulonimbus et que sais-je encore … Cette fois je suis bien décidé, nous irons faire un tour en planeur dès que nous aurons pris le dessert.

– Mais, Monsieur le Curé, vous n'avez pas peur de monter dans un planeur ?

– Voyons, Mademoiselle, auriez-vous peur de monter au ciel ?

– Que Nenni, Monsieur le Curé, j'aurais plutôt peur de voler par terre.

– Qu'en pensez-vous père Paul ?

– Ma foi, la poésie et l'exaltation du vol libre ne doivent pas faire oublier les dures lois de la physique …

– Père Paul, j'en ai assez des lourdeurs de la vie et des pesanteurs de la physique. Allons-y, larguons les amarres et, dans le pire des cas, nous compterons sur votre absolution!

– Ah Monsieur le Neveu, quel bel oiseau! Il fait au moins vingt mètres celui-là … Mais si vous le voulez bien, je vois qu'il y a deux sièges, je prendrai celui de devant. Il me semble ainsi que nous serons bien lestés de l'avant ? C'est ce qu'il faut n'est-ce pas ?

– Il ne faudrait pas que, une fois en l'air, moi à l'arrière, nous partions subitement en marche arrière … Dites- moi, ce serait dangereux ?

– Ma foi, Monsieur le Curé, avec cette machine, une fois qu'on a enclenché la marche arrière, il n'y a plus moyen de revenir en en arrière, si j'ose dire.

– C'est ainsi que nous pourrions en quelque sorte entrer au paradis à reculons ? N'est-ce pas, c'est bien cela, que vous voulez dire ?

– Oui, c'est bien cela, Monsieur le Curé, mais je suis persuadé que vous préférez y aller en marche avant, la vue est bien meilleure ; surtout quand on se rapproche de cette maudite terre que l'on va bientôt quitter. Ainsi regardez devant, mon ami Michel est en train de mettre un anneau, attaché à un câble, dans le nez de notre oiseau. Nous serons ensuite remorqués à plus de cinq cents mètres par ce gros biplan que vous voyez devant nous.

– Ah, mon Dieu, quand je pense à ma sainte mère qui m'interdisait même de regarder les avions dans le ciel … elle disait qu'il y avait ww de choses à voir sur terre, il est vrai que j'avais toujours la tête en l'air, ha, ha, ha …

– Pensait-elle que le paradis est sur terre et que l'enfer serait au ciel ?

– Je ne sais trop que penser, mais regardez voilà que le biplan qui se met à rouler!

– Eh oui, Monsieur le Curé, accrochez-vous, car bientôt il va voler … et nous derrière lui.

– Dans le fond, cet avion remorqueur n'est- il pas un cheval de trait ? Il me fait penser au cheval ailé, vous voyez ce que je veux dire, Monsieur le Neveu.

– Je suppose que vous voulez parler de Pégase, mais je dois avouer, Monsieur le Curé, que ma culture équestre est plutôt terre à terre ; mais avez-vous senti que nous venions de quitter la planète terre ?

- Oui, c'est bien de lui qu'il s'agit, de Pégase, le cheval ailé qui devient la monture de Zeus lui-même … Ah, Monsieur le neveu, nous filons vers l'Olympe tiré par le cheval de Zeus lui-même … Que voulez-vous de plus ?

- Bien, Monsieur le Curé, il ne faudrait pas que la corde casse ; que notre cheval meure de soif et ne veuille plus avancer ou que sais-je encore ?

- Ah non, Monsieur le Neveu, vous n'allez pas me dire que ce cheval est parti l'estomac vide … dans ce cas-là, je comprendrais qu'il nous fausse compagnie …

- Vous voulez dire qu'il nous entraînerait avec lui … vers le bas?

- Nous l'aurions mérité, on ne laisse pas partir un cheval même ailé l'estomac vide, cela ne se fait pas … et c'est même dangereux. Nous par contre, si je me souviens bien, nous avons pris nos précautions ; je ne sais plus au juste combien de bouteilles nous avons bues, à vue de nez je dirais deux Aloxe-Corton et deux Pontet-Canet, le décompte vous parait—il correct ?

- Je suis comme vous, Monsieur le Curé, je ne me souviens plus très bien, mais il me semble que vous pourriez ajouter un Gevrey Chambertin, sans compter le champagne.

- Ah oui, c'est vrai ; je ne compte jamais les bouteilles de champagne … c'est sans doute parce qu'elles ne sont pas millésimées, ha, ha, ha.

- Monsieur le Curé, nous allons bientôt devoir quitter notre cheval ailé. Il va retourner à l'écurie; nous allons donc devoir nous débrouiller sans lui …

– Mon Dieu, c'est effrayant, ce que vous me dites, nous serons donc seuls abandonnés dans l'éther ?

– Pas vraiment abandonnés, Monsieur le Curé, la Providence, si vous voyez ce que je veux dire, nous pouvons compter sur elle, n'est-ce pas ? Oui, c'est cela, parlons-en ; mais que peut-elle nous apporter dans l'immédiat ?

– Là tout de suite, je verrais bien la Providence sous la forme d'un puissant courant ascendant qui nous ferait grimper dans l'éther, un peu comme un ascenseur à l'intérieur duquel on continuerait t à voler, le nez pointé vers le bas …

– Oui, ça, j'ai bien compris, le nez pointé vers la bas, jamais vers le haut, cela il faut l'éviter à tout prix … mais revenons à nos moutons.

– Justement, il nous faudrait des moutons, des moutons blancs dans un ciel bleu, je veux dire des cumuli.

– Ah, quel vol magnifique, des oiseaux, des chevaux ailés, des moutons blancs, je crois entendre le lied de la Vie Céleste de Mahler.

– De qui ?

– De Mahler, 4ème symphonie, 4ème mouvement, écoutez plutôt !

Nous goûtons les joies célestes
Détournés des choses terrestres
Du ciel on n'entend guère le tumulte du monde
Tout vit dans la paix la plus douce
Nous menons une vie angélique
Mais qu'elle n'est pas notre gaîté

> *Nous dansons et bondissons*
> *Nous volons et chantons.*

- N'est-ce pas merveilleux?
- Je pense, Monsieur le Curé, que le tumulte du monde se rapproche de nous ; nous ne sommes plus qu'à deux cents mètres, il va falloir songer à reprendre goût à la vie sur terre.
- Ah non, nous n'allons pas laisser tomber les bras. Regardez devant vous, il y a le petit bois du village le bien nommé Bost, foncez vers lui, la Providence nous y attend !
- Nous y allons toutes voiles dehors, Monsieur le Curé, mais nous n'avons déjà plus que cent cinquante mètres.
- Monsieur le Neveu, vous n'êtes qu'un petit comptable, vous me décevez : réduisez votre vitesse, inclinez un peu à gauche, non, encore un peu plus, réduisez encore la vitesse, pas de trop ; braquez maintenant franchement à gauche et attendez …
- On dirait que cela veut monter.
- Homme de peu de foi, maintenez votre inclinaison et votre vitesse, appuyez encore à gauche et, pendant que vous travaillez la machine, je vais ajouter, si vous le voulez bien, quelques vers au chant de Mahler:

> *L'éther se soulève pour nous*
> *Sans bruit, sans fureur*
> *Nous planons, nous montons,*
> *En lui, nous baignons sans peur.*

– Oui, mais Monsieur le Curé, nous ne montons plus guère; nous allons bientôt toucher la cime des arbres …

– Mais, Monsieur le Neveu, vous et moi ne sommes-nous pas faits pour vivre sur les cimes ?

– Si fait, mais tout à côté, il y a le cimetière …

– Bon, puisque c'est comme ça, virez une dernière fois à gauche, n'oubliez pas d'incliner et de mettre un peu de pied, prenez le cap 06, voyez si la piste est libre, surveillez votre vitesse, attention à la route, … ensuite, laissez rouler la machine au sol jusqu'à l'arrêt complet.

– Voilà nous sommes à terre, nous sommes sauvés …

– Ah, Monsieur le Neveu, laissez-moi achever ce vol mémorable en vous redisant ce quatrain mutatis mutandis:

> *Nous goûtions les joies célestes*
> *Détournés des choses terrestres*
> *Du ciel on n'entendait guère*
> *Le tumulte du monde …*

Quatrain, auquel j'ajouterai, si vous le voulez bien avant de quitter l'oiseau blanc, le tercet suivant :

> *Bienheureux le Seigneur*
> *Qui après l'ascension*
> *A pu garder les hauteurs …*

ASCENSION

– Well, miss, I am tired of hearing your nephew tell us about updrafts, cumulus clouds, stratus clouds, cumulonimbus clouds, and God only knows what else. This time, I've made up my mind. We're going to go for a ride in a glider. Right after dessert.

– But, Father, aren't you afraid of going up in a glider?

– Would you be afraid of going up to heaven, miss?

– No way, Father. I would be afraid to fly on the ground.

– What do you think about this, Father Paul?

– Well, poetry and the excitement of free flight should not make us forget the harsh rules of physics.

– Well, I have enough of the burdens of life and the heaviness of physics, Father Paul. So let's go for it. Anchors aweigh. If worse comes to worst, we can always count on our absolution.

– What a fine bird this is, young man. At least twenty meters. I see that there are two seats. If you don't mind, I'll take the one in front. That way, we'll be nicely ballasted up front, no? That's what we need, isn't it? Otherwise, we risk that once airborne, with me in the back, we'll suddenly go in reverse … Tell me, would it be dangerous?

– Why, Father, once we engage the reverse rear in this baby, there's no going back, I dare say.

– So that's how we could get into heaven … Backward, as it were? Isn't that what you wanted to say?

– That's exactly it, Father. But I'm convinced you'd rather go forward. The view is far better, particularly when we draw close to this accursed earth that we are about to leave. So, have a look up front. My friend Michel is putting on a ring attached to a rope in our bird's nose. We are going to be towed to more than five hundred meters high by this large biplane you see in front of you.

- Good Lord … when I think that my saintly mother had forbidden me to look at planes in the sky. She used to say that there were enough things to see here on Earth. It's true that I always had my head in the clouds. Ha, ha, ha.
- Did she think that heaven was on Earth and hell in heaven?
- I do not know what to make of it all, but look … the biplane is on the move.
- Indeed it is, Father. Hold tight because it will take off soon, and we will fly behind it.
- When you think about it, isn't this towing plane a draught horse of sorts? It makes me think of that winged horse, if you see what I mean.
- I suppose you are referring to Pegasus, but I must admit, Father, that my understanding of horses is rather down-to-earth. Incidentally, did you feel that we've just left planet Earth behind us?
- Yes, that's the one, Pegasus, that Zeus himself would ride. We are heading for Olympus by Zeus's own horse. What more could you want?
- Well, Father, let's hope that the rope does not break and that the horse is not thirsty and refuses to budge … that sort of thing.

- You are not going to tell me that this horse has set off on an empty stomach, are you? In that case, I would understand that he'd want to part company.

- You mean draw us down ... along with it?

- We would have deserved it too. You simply don't let a horse set off on an empty stomach. It's even dangerous. We, as I recall, took our precautions; I can no longer remember how many bottles we downed. Off the top of my head, I would say two Aloxe Corton and two Pontet Canet ... What do you say?

- I do not recall too well either, Father, but I think you could add a Gevrey Chambertin, not counting the champagne.

- Right, now that you mention it. I never count the bottles of champagne ... no doubt because they were not vintage years. Ha, ha, ha.

- We will soon have to leave our winged horse, Father. He will go back to the stable, and we will have to make do without him.

- Good God, what you say frightens me. You mean we are going to be abandoned in the ether?

- Not really abandoned, Father. We can always count on Providence, if you see what I mean.

- Right ... Providence. Let's talk about it. But what can Providence do for us here and now?

- Well, right now I would welcome Providence in the form of a powerful updraft that would help us climb in the ether, something like an elevator inside which we would continue to fly, with the nose pointed down.

- Yes, I get it, the nose pointed down, never up. We must avoid that at all times. But let's get back to our sheep, as we say.
- That's precisely what we would need ... sheep ... white sheep against a blue sky. I mean cumulus clouds.
- Ah, what a marvelous flight. Birds, winged horses, white sheep ... I think I can hear "The Heavenly Life" by Mahler.
- By whom?
- Mahler, fourth symphony, forth movement. Just listen.

We enjoy heavenly pleasures
And therefore avoid earthly ones.
No worldly tumult is to be heard in heaven.
We all live in greatest peace
We lead angelic lives,
Yet have a merry time of it besides.
We dance and we spring,
we skip and sing.

- Isn't it just marvelous? What do you think?
- I think that the worldly tumult is drawing near us, Father ... We are just two hundred meters away now. We'll have to rediscover a taste for earthly life.
- Well, we're not going to give up now, just like that. Look in front of you. There is the little forest of the village ... the property called Bost. Head straight for it. Providence awaits us.

–   We are heading at full speed, Father, but there are only a hundred and fifty meters left …

–   Young man, you are talking like a petty accountant. I am disappointed in you. Reduce your speed, lean a bit left … no, some more … a little bit more. Reduce the speed again … not too much. Now veer sharply left and wait.

–   You'd think it wants to go up …

–   Oh ye of little faith, steady with your incline and speed. Press a little more to the left, and while you are working the machine, I will add some verses from Mahler's song.

> *The ether arises for us*
> *Without sound, without fury,*
> *We glide, we rise,*
> *And bathe in it fearlessly.*

–   Yes, that's fine, Father, but we are no longer rising. We will soon touch the peaks of the trees.

–   But aren't you and I made to live on the peaks?

–   Well enough, but the cemetery is right next to them.

–   Well, if that's the case, turn left one last time. Do not forget to tilt and put a little weight into it. Take course zero six. See whether the runway is free. Watch your speed. Keep your eyes on the road. Then just let the machine roll on the ground until it comes to a standstill.

- There we are. Back on Earth, safe and sound.
- Ah, young man, let me bring this memorable flight to a close by repeating this quatrain with slight changes to suit the occasion.

> *We enjoyed heavenly pleasures*
> *And therefore avoided earthly ones.*
> *No worldly tumult*
> *Was to be heard in heaven.*

- And, before we leave this white bird, I would like to add the following tercet.

Blessed is the lord
Who after the ascension
Managed to stay aloft.

DE NATURA RERUM

Father Paul, I would like to take advantage of this quiet moment when the children are in the garden to talk to you about a question that has been bugging me for many years. Since 1959, to be precise …

- Why 1959?
- Well, that's the year I put together my wine cellar.
- Ah yes. That's true. You only have wine from '59 … But what is the question?
- Well, Father Paul, as far back as I can look into the past, with the exception of the Far East, where people like to drink tea, literature has always feted wine as a divine drink or, in any event, as the nectar or beverage of the gods. So here is my question. Is wine a divine creation or simply something that the gods, which means men, discovered?
- Well, Father, that's a very delicate question that the Council of Trent took great care to avoid, in spite of the insistence of a Polish bishop, who if my memory does not fail me was called Maximus Picolus. The Pope refused to address an issue that was not on the agenda.
- The issue was not on the agenda?
- Father, I know that you were a vicar in a municipality with special arrangements for the two language communities, but is that reason enough to use this "issue," which smells corked, and this "agenda," which stems from the same barrel?
- Well, Father Paul, I know you are a purist, and that is the reason I have come to you. So if I understood correctly,

the Council of Trent, or any subsequent council for that matter, examined the issue. The question remains open.

- Yes, that's it. We can talk about it freely without any fear of sanction, but bearing in mind nonetheless that we are not permitted just any opinion whatsoever.

- Of course, of course. We are not going to publish the outcome of our discussion ... At least not at once. It will have to pass the test of time first.

- Well, let us get to the crux of the matter, since you have called on me. The question must obviously be placed in the broader context of creation. Now, I fear lest we be bound in the creationist hypothesis, if I may call it that ...

- Well, that goes without saying, but we cannot overlook the determinist hypothesis or the theory of evolution and of natural selection ...

- When I hear you speak, Father, I fear that we must staysail "close hauled" to avoid any formidable pitfalls.

- Father Paul, on the creationist front, which is our article of faith, it is highly unlikely nonetheless that at the end of the seventh day Adam managed to find finely pruned vine stocks aged thirty to forty years, ready to produce the finest wine.

- I think that's right. But the question is not framed in those terms, but as follows, in my view: Were all the ingredients necessary for the subsequent emergence of our divine beverage already available in the seventh day of creation?

- I would like to draw your attention to the fact that you are falling into the deterministic rut, Father Paul. As you see it, everything was designed in advance.
- The deterministic rut may just be a divine expression after all. But of course, let us not fall into pantheism. God is not in everything. For that matter, the line of thought I am suggesting does not stand in the way of including the most recent theories. If these are to be believed, life originated in the oceans and the first living organisms that evolved landed up on our beaches in some way. Well, you will see that in my view, the evolution of our favorite beverage will follow that of the species step-by-step.
- I do not see what you are getting at.
- I feel obliged to give you an example to get across what I am trying to say. Have you ever considered why we prefer white wine chilled to a red wine when having seafood?
- Because it goes better?
- The answer seems a little short, Father. Just think of the fact that the fish is the first living being of a certain size to have wound up on land and then have evolved into other terrestrial forms of life. The fish is a cold-blooded vertebrate that will evolve to other species said to be cold-blooded. The fish shares with white wine the fact that it is the result of a first rapid draft … You are no doubt aware that white wine is the result of a rapid pressing, unlike red wine, which requires prior fermentation. For my part, I see a clear parallel between the evolution of cold-blooded species to warm-blooded species and the evolution from

white wine to the grand red wines that you are ever so fond of—and rightly so, I might add.

- You mean to say, Father Paul, that red wine is the fruit of the patience and genius of the gods, who understood that the grape had to be left to ferment in a vat before drawing wine?

- That's exactly what I mean. Nature first created cold-blooded living beings—those we enjoy with a chilled wine—and warm-blooded mammals evolved afterward. They are the gems of creation, and the best species are comparable to the great vintage wines. They are read and enjoyed at the right temperature.

- Yes. That's very true, Father Paul. After all, a great wine is said to have body, is ropy, and has the color of pigeon's blood, etc. There, Father, you are alluding to an accessory that is in no way indispensable, at least as far as a good wine is concerned.

- Yes, but that brings us far from our philosophical preoccupations; I would say even theological insofar as we are deliberating on the basis of creation. Without overlooking the attainments of modern theories ...

- And in the same line of thinking, you see a relation between the color of a great red wine and the color of ornaments of our church prelates and senior magistrates?

- It takes people of high quality to appreciate everything that creation can give us. As to the color red that they wear on special occasions, they simply want to remind us that they are men and not cold-blooded fish.

- But then why is His Holiness the Pope always dressed in white?

- I would venture, Father, without claiming the benefit of infallibility in any way, that our Holy Father wants to serve as a reminder of the possible great ravages of great vintages that have turned, and the virtue of young wine for those whose tastes and duties could lead to immoderate consumption.

- And yet it is a divine beverage?

- Why, certainly, Father. But we sometimes get the impression that things happen as if the creator had lost control of evolution.

BELGIAN DENTISTS

When we got out of the airport, she hailed a taxi driver and said briefly, "Fifty-six boulevard Malombré."

"Is that the dental clinic?" asked the driver.

"Yes, it is.

"Good … And where are you from? Myself, I am Portuguese."

"So you are not a native … And we, we come from Belgium. We are Belgian dentists."

"Oh, Belgian dentists," he said. "If I had known that you were Belgian dentists, I would have guessed that you were going not to the clinic but to the bank."

"Ah, we don't understand."

"Don't take it badly, but let me explain that in this country Belgian dentists have a special reputation."

"And which reputation?"

"They are said to make big money selling false teeth and driving here to hide good money in our safes."

"Do you mean that the Malombré dental clinic is a bank?"

"Not at all, so far as I am well informed. I wanted only to make clear that if I had at first known that you were dentists, I would have guessed that you were not going to the dental clinic but to the bank on the same block. Do you understand?"

"We didn't know that we had such a reputation. Thank you very much for this information, but let us tell you that we don't have any money in our bags but very special surgical devices that we are going to use at this clinic."

"So you are specialists?"

"Sort of. You could say that. In fact, we travel all over Europe to perform very specific operations. Yesterday, we were in Berlin.

Tomorrow we will be in Dresden, and the day after that Leningrad. Last week we were in Paris, Bergen, and Brussels."

"Very hard work?"

"And dangerous too."

"Dangerous?"

"Of course. Every day we take a new taxi and we don't know anything about the drivers. We are forced to have full confidence in them. On the contrary, our patients are waiting for us, knowing perfectly who we are and what and how we are going to perform."

"So you have returning customers?"

"Not at all. When we visit a dental clinic, we don't come back a second time. We are, as we say, the sort of artists who do not perform two times at the same place. We are too famous and too busy to come back in a city previously visited, except of course New York, London, Paris, or Beijing, or even Mumbai …"

"Did you operate in China, or even in India?"

"Of course, but we don't like to suffer long flights anymore, so we prefer now to limit our business—if we can speak of business— to Europe and North Africa."

"Is it the first time you have come to our city?"

"Yes, and probably the last time. As we told you before, we never come back to the same place twice."

"I suppose that you perform very specific operations and that you have some sort of patent preventing somebody from challenging your business."

"You know, our practice is a very old one and is inspired by the old Egyptian dentists of five thousand years ago."

"My colleague," continues the lady, "is a specialist of old Egypt. During a visit ten years ago to Shakarra, he could decipher inside the pyramid how the old Egyptian dentists operated to extract teeth, put them right, even drill holes to insert implants, and so on."

"Do you mean that you are performing in the old way, ignoring the modern techniques?"

"Absolutely," she said without hesitation.

"I am surprised," said the Portuguese taxi driver. "I can't believe it."

"Why not try? Remember, we won't come a second time to your city. It is the first and last appearance of us in this town. Have you a special problem in your mouth? We could clear it up in the Egyptian way."

"What is the Egyptian way?"

"The Egyptian way is the most daring experience a dentist can do in his or her life. Look at my colleague's fingers."

"I can't see them because I am driving and do not want to end up at the hospital with two Egyptian dentists with French names."

"Yes, look ahead. I can describe to you exactly how his fingers are."

"How are they?"

"They are one centimeter shorter than yours."

"You mean that they are shortened in order to work more easily in the patient's mouth?"

"I wouldn't say that," said the lady. "In fact, it is easiest to handle a client's mouth with long and slim fingers like mine. That is the reason we work together. We form a team, each of us with special skills according to the needs of the patient."

"I am completely surprised," said the taxi driver. "I don't understand why you rely on ancient practices when we have at our disposal the accurate and new techniques of today."

"That is the heart of the matter," she answered. "Have you ever heard of people who cannot support or receive analgesics? If you inject them with analgesics, they could die immediately in the dentist chair. It occurred to me twice in my previous life."

"And then?"

"And then we had to perform like the Egyptians, as they did five thousand years ago. So, if you want to try—we just arrived at the dental clinic—we could extract your bad teeth in two minutes or, if you prefer, drill a hole in your maxillaries in half an hour."

"Without pain?

"Who said without pain? My colleague or me?"

"Do you think, little man, that we could do this job without pain? Look at my colleague's fingers. Look at them. The first was taken away by a priest, the second by a movie star, and the third by a newborn."

"Yes, sir, by a newborn," said the man accompanying the lady. "I was contacted by an obstetrician, a friend of mine. He told me a scan had revealed that a pregnant woman had in her womb a baby with complete dentition. He had never seen that and asked me to assist him at the birth. Now, five years later, I don't know who—the mother or the baby—took off my third finger."

"I was asking without pain for the patient?"

"There is nothing without pain on this planet," said the lady, "but listen, there are ways to lessen the pain."

"How?"

"For us it is very simple. The patients know they cannot go on analgesics. Their current practitioners don't want to do the job. It's too dangerous, and in any event they are going to lose the patients. So they fetch us to do the dirty job. Our trick is to ask astronomical fees. They are so high that for this price the patient is pretty sure that he is not going to endure pain. So he comes like a sheep. If the price is high enough, he would never suffer; we only ask him to recount mentally the amount of money he gave us … before starting the job, of course. Sometimes, the trick fails, and it is the reason you can see the shortened fingers of my colleague, and my nose. I had to receive surgery two years ago."

"Oh my God," said the taxi driver. "It is unbelievable."

"Yes, it is," said the lady. "And don't tell this story to anybody. No one will believe you. On the other hand," she said, "our patients don't tell anyone about their ordeals because they would be ashamed for having paid so much … to a bunch of butchers. You now understand why we don't come back, even for a holiday, in a town where we performed so adequately. We could be shot dead by an angry old patient."

As I was going to pay the taxi driver, we saw somebody enter the dental clinic. She gave a weird smile to the driver. He was so frightened that he pulled off without taking his fare.

"Fine day," she said. "Let's go to work. Our plane is at four."

AFRICAN SHOES

His name is Oxford. He is not English but Greek. He has very dark hair and is in his midfifties. He runs a small shoe repair shop and a shoe shop in a narrow commercial gangway under an apartment block. On the other side of the passage there is a storeroom and another glass cabinet.

So, like a waiter in a French brasserie, he is always running from one place to another in a desperate effort to satisfy all his clients and friends.

He has a clerk to help him sell the shoes, and two aides in the repair shop, where you can also buys keys and find help if you have lost your keys. They will accompany you to your house and open the doors with the adequate materials (drills, etc.).

The sales clerk, whose name is Maryse, is Mauritian. The two aides are Moroccans.

"It's little Africa," he would say later.

When I entered the shop, I saw in this small place one counter and three chairs. Maryse was idle behind the counter. In front of her, along the wall, sat a man in his thirties and his pregnant wife. I would later come to know that they were expecting a boy, due the next week. They didn't talk; they seemed to be waiting quietly for the end of the day.

Not wanting to wait even five minutes, I tried to go back out, to escape, but Oxford came in behind me. I had the feeling now that from his repair shop he had seen that I was not only hesitating to enter but also willing to desert the place.

He is a very gifted merchant and actor. He said, "Take this place"—the only chair left—"and I will care for you immediately."

At this time I didn't know, of course, that I was going to spend two and a half hours seated on this uncomfortable armchair.

Oxford disappeared because somebody had entered the shoe repair shop and he didn't have faith in the capacity of his two aides to retain the clients even for a small repair.

Maryse, the architect (the father-to-be was an architect), and his wife remained silent, but they looked happy and comfortable.

I got up and said I was going to examine the glass cabinet on the other side of the passage. In fact, I was considering escaping anew when Oxford, abandoning another client in his repair shop, was once more behind me and said, "Come on. I am just free for you."

I reentered the shop and sat back down on the uncomfortable chair.

"You need, at first sight," he said, "a size forty, forty and a half. Maryse, will you ask monsieur what he wants and bring him some pairs. After that, I'll come to see what's the best for him."

He disappeared anew, and I tried to explain to her very briefly and clearly what I needed. She left the shop and entered the storage room through the lobby, going through to the apartments. I began to realize that she knew nearly everybody weaving in all directions when crossing the gangway.

I stayed alone with the architect and his pregnant wife.

"I am a returning customer," I said. "The first time I came here, perhaps ten years ago, it was already a little bit strange, but now it is a real mess."

"Yes, it's true," replied the architect. "That is why we took this afternoon off. Now they are polishing my boots. It is time consuming, but it will be extremely well done."

After what seemed to me like an hour or two, Maryse came back with three boxes. She opened the boxes, and I said immediately, "I was sure that you didn't listen to what I said. You have brought me just the opposite of what I want."

Despite the noises of the polishing machine, Oxford sensed from a distance that the atmosphere was disintegrating. He came in when Maryse left the room.

"I am desperate," he said. "She is not professional, she does what she likes, she doesn't respect the client … and so on."

He seemed so friendly and like he was seeking advice and solace, so I said, "Why don't get you rid of her?"

"I think about it," he replied, and he left me alone, saying he was going to fetch the shoes I deserved himself, special shoes for men with flat feet, a condition that caused foot ache and eventually lumbago.

Maryse reentered the room, and she said, "He is a difficult man. He is never satisfied. I am considering finding another job. I would like to sell clothes to women."

"He is a fine man," I said very patiently. "You'll never find the same."

At this moment, Mrs. Dumont, a resident of the third floor, came in and began to interfere in our conversation.

"So you have aching feet," she said. "Me too." She began to show me her feet, how bad they were, how she needed new shoes, and so on.

When Oxford came back, she decided to leave, and she came to me to shake hands.

"Excuse me," I said. "I have severe lumbago, and I can hardly stand up to shake your hand." Nevertheless, I tried to get up, letting her see my back pain.

Five minutes later, she entered the shop again; she exchanged some words with Maryse and then left the place.

"She came back," said Maryse, "because you made her laugh with your lumbago. In fact, she is looking for a man."

"Oh, I am very surprised," I said.

"Are you married?" she asked.

I hesitated before answering and eventually said, not giving more explanation, "I live alone."

"Oh fine," she replied. "That is great. I am going to call Mrs Dumont back immediately so you can invite her for dinner in the restaurant next door."

"No, no, please," I said as she was proceeding to the telephone. "I forbid you to call her."

Oxford came back with the polished boots and showed them to the architect. It took him ten minutes to admire the polish, ask recommendations for further polishing at home, and ask his pregnant wife to jot down what Oxford said about polishing with white cream and polishing devices.

They eventually left the shop.

"You know," said Maryse, "Monsieur Renard met Mrs. Dumont and has refused to have dinner with her. Nevertheless, I am going to call Mrs. Dumont." She proceeded to the telephone again.

"No, no," I said. "Don't call her. I won't."

"But, Maryse," said Oxford, "it's not your business. Mr. Renard is perhaps married."

"No, no, he lives alone," she said.

"That is quite different," said Oxford. "What do you have to lose if you meet Mrs. Dumont in the restaurant next door?"

"No, no," I said. "I came to buy new shoes, have them wrapped up, pay, and then get back home for a quiet evening."

Just then, another man in his forties entered the scene. He was well dressed with magnificent brown shoes that were polished as if they were brand new. He seated himself in the chair abandoned by the pregnant wife and began to smile at Maryse, who stayed idle behind her counter.

Then she left us again.

"What a mess here," I said.

"Oh yes," he said. "One must be accustomed to come here to buy something."

We began to talk.

He was a sales manager. His company sold windows. So we spoke about windows, the different kinds of wood, and plastic windows. He lived in a suburb of the city in a house with a garden, lawns, mower, and perhaps a wife and children.

Once again, Oxford reappeared with different shoe boxes. Maryse followed him with a tray that held three glass of white wine that she had just bought next door.

When showing me the shoes I am now wearing, Oxford said, "You know, Mrs. Dumont is very smart. She likes that you travel. She is sort of an intellectual. You don't have anything to lose by meeting her. Why not try? But, if you prefer, on the third floor there is Ghislaine."

"Oh, yes, Ghislaine," said Maryse.

Oxford glanced carefully at me and said, "She is a little taller than you, not too much, but she is well off. It is very important, if you see what I mean."

"Oh yes," said Maryse. "I am calling Ghislaine right now." She went anew to fetch the telephone book.

"No, no," I said. "I want to get back home as soon as possible. I must feed my cats."

"Oh," said Maryse. "On the seventh floor we have also the widow of the pharmacist, about sixty, good-looking."

"Yes," said Oxford, "the widow of the pharmacist who died last year. We have his telephone number."

"Yes, I am calling her right now," she said.

I feared the lady would actually come and I would find myself trapped. So in need of desperate maneuvers to escape this marketplace, I said, "No, no. I said I want to pay for my shoes and get back home to mow my lawn."

Oxford said, "If you cannot choose between the two pairs you like best, I advice you to buy the two, and I will give you a discount of fifty euros."

"Yes," I said, "I can buy the two pairs but with a discount of hundred."

"No, that is impossible," said Oxford, "but let me emphasize once again the fact that you must consider having lunch or dinner with Ghislaine, or the pharmacist's wife, or even with Mrs. Dumont."

"No, no," I said. Then, wanting to get rid of them, I said loudly, "I am not interested at all." And turning to my second desperate maneuver, as the first had failed, I added, "And to tell you the truth, I would prefer a man."

Then Maryse came in front of me smiling widely, showing the white protruding teeth of an African woman, and said confidentially, "The shoes you chose match very well with the ones Marcel wears." She was referring to the guy behind me (the windows sales manager).

I pretended not to hear or understand what she said. "I was very happy to have met Michel," I said. I got up and went to the counter, asking to pay.

"How much do you want to pay?" Maryse said.

"What?"

"You tell me how much you want to pay … I can give you a special discount."

"I made a deal with your boss," I said. "I want to pay what was agreed, and you are a fool. If your boss should learn about that, he could get rid of you."

She smiled maliciously when Oxford entered the shop. Once more he had sensed from a distance that something was going wrong with Maryse.

"What are you doing?" he asked her.

I was on the verge of saying, "It's not me. It's your clerk who wanted to renegotiate the deal." Instead I said, "I want to pay, have my shoes wrapped, and get back home."

I made sure that Oxford himself put the right shoes in the right boxes, fearing I would discover at home a pair of boots or something else.

I shook hands with Marcel. Maryse had yet again vanished.

In the gangway, Oxford came up once more behind me and said, "It is Africa. I am exhausted. And the two Moroccans, have you seen them working?"

"The first thing to do," I said, "is to get rid of Maryse. She doesn't help you. She gives you more work."

"Yes, I know," he said. "But the fact is that she is thirty-four, and I have lived with her for nine years."

"Oh," I replied. "I understand. You have lost the controls."

"Yes, I lost the controls two weeks after she came to live with me, and the problem is that we can't divorce, for we are not married."

"Oh, I see you are a very special lawyer. In this country, where we are, people don't get married in order to avoid divorce, and in your country people don't divorce because they are not married," I said. "Tell me, how long will my new shoes last?"

"At least ten years. They are premium quality," he answered.

"Okay, I got two pairs, so I'll come back to your shop in twenty years."

"No, no," he said. "We sell socks, and you deserve a very good pair of black shoes, even two. You bought only brown ones."

"And what about Michel?" I asked. "Is he a customer? I have the feeling that he came only to see your nonworking wife behind the counter."

"No," he replied. "He comes each Saturday in the afternoon. He stays on a chair, smiling to Maryse, hoping to meet a man buying shoes. It is a very good place to meet men, you know."

"Oh, I didn't realize that. And the widows?" I asked.

"They flock to the shop, with Maryse's connivance," he said, "when they see a man of your age inside. I would be glad to get rid of them."

"So marry them," I said, "so you could get a divorce."

CPSIA information can be obtained at www.ICGtesting.com
Printed in the USA
LVOW11s1737140815

450056LV00003B/252/P